THE Berenstain BEAR SCOUTS

Ghost versus Ghost

D0169854

THE Berenstain BEAR SCOUTS

Ghost versus Ghost

by Stan & Jan Berenstain
Illustrated by Michael Berenstain

A
LITTLE APPLE
PAPERBACK

SCHOLASTIC INC.
New York Toronto London Auckland Sydney

ISBN 0-590-60386-8

12 11 10 9 8 7 6   9/9 0 1/0

Printed in the U.S.A.   40

First Scholastic printing, October 1996

• Table of Contents •

THE Berenstain BEAR SCOUTS

Ghost versus Ghost

• Chapter 1 •

Scout Leader Jane Says No

The Bear Scouts were surprised. It was the first time Scout Leader Jane had ever turned them down on a merit badge. When the scouts told her the next badge they wanted to try for, she reached for the *Official Bear Scout Handbook* that was always on her desk. She opened it to the section on merit badges and read silently for what seemed like a long time but was really less than a minute. Then she snapped the book shut and said, "Scouts, there's no way I'm going to let you try for the Wilderness Survival Merit Badge."

The scouts were not only surprised,
they were disappointed. Except for Sister.
She was relieved. She knew that the
Wilderness Survival Merit Badge would

have to be earned in the forest across the river—the Great Grizzly Forest, otherwise known as the *Haunted* Forest.

Not that Sister believed in ghosts. But somehow she was afraid of them anyway. That's the way it is with ghosts. They're scary whether you believe in them or not. That's the way it was with Sister as well. She was probably the bravest member of the troop. Except where ghosts were concerned. The other scouts knew about Sister's touchiness about ghosts and that she was nervous about going into Great Grizzly Forest.

Brother wasn't ready to take "no" for an answer. "Why won't you let us try for the Wildnerness Survival Merit Badge?" said Brother. "We've earned some pretty tough badges: the Rock-climbing Badge and the Scuba-diving Badge, to name two."

"Right," said Fred. "The Wilderness

Survival Merit Badge sounds really interesting."

"We might see some animals we've never seen before," said Lizzy.

"And some ghosts," said Sister under her breath.

"There are three reasons why I can't permit you to try for the Wilderness Survival Merit Badge," said Jane. She held up three fingers and ticked off the reasons. "One: Rock climbing and scuba diving are tea parties compared to surviving in the wilderness. And don't forget, Professor Actual Factual was with you on those badges. I don't think it's fair for you to go running to Actual Factual every time you have a merit-badge problem. Two: Great Grizzly Forest, which is our only true wilderness, is on the other side of Great Roaring River. So you couldn't even get there if I gave you the go-ahead to try for the badge. And three: You don't know a blessed thing about surviving in the wilderness."

"But we're experienced campers," said Brother.

"We've camped out overnight," said Fred.

"Lots of times," said Lizzy.

"Hey, gang," said Sister, "there are other badges we could try for."

"We earned our Camp-out Badges months ago," said Brother.

"We've got all kinds of camping gear," said Fred.

"We've got tents, stoves, fishing gear— all kinds of stuff," said Lizzy.

"There's the Basket-weaving Badge, the Mapmaking badge, the Flower-pressing Badge," said Sister.

Scouts Brother, Fred, and Lizzy turned and glared at Sister.

"Your problem," said Lizzy, "is that you

believe all that silly stuff about Great
Grizzly Forest being haunted."

"No I don't," said Sister.

"Yes you do," said Lizzy.

"No I don't!" said Sister.

"Yes you do!" said Lizzy.

"Well," said Sister. "I'll tell you one
thing I'm *not* afraid of. And that's you!"

Sister and Lizzy were best friends. But
they did have their differences from time
to time.

"Now, now," said Jane. "We must learn
to respect each other's fears and concerns.

But it's not ghosts that are the problem with the Wilderness Survival Merit Badge. The problem is that your tents, your stoves, your fishing gear, and all your other camping equipment aren't going to be of any use to you in Great Grizzly Forest."

"Why not?" said Brother.

"Because you can't take your camping gear into the wilderness with you," said Jane.

"Huh?" said Brother.

"Obviously, you haven't taken the trouble to read what the *Bear Scout Guide* says about the Wilderness Survival Merit Badge," said Jane.

She was right. Brother was embarrassed. He usually made it his business to be prepared. But he'd gotten so excited about the idea of the Wilderness Badge that he'd leaped before he looked.

Jane had reopened the handbook and was reading. "To earn the Wilderness Survival Merit Badge, a scout must meet the following conditions. One: The scout must spend at least twenty-four hours in the wilderness. Two: The scout must enter the wilderness without provisions—this includes food and water. . . ."

No food and water? The scouts could hardly believe their ears. They started to ask questions. But Jane held her hand up to stop them. She read on: "Three: The scout may take only the following items into the wilderness: one Bear Scout uniform, one Bear Scout sleeping bag, one Bear Scout ax, and one Bear Scout collapsible metal cup."

"That's all?" said Brother. "The clothes on our back, a sleeping bag, an ax, and a collapsible metal cup?"

"Good grief!" said Fred. "No food! No water! No tent! No way to catch fish! How are we supposed to survive?"

"Oh, yes," said Jane. "There's one other

thing you are permitted to take: an Official Bear Scouts' First Aid Kit."

"Great," said Fred. "That'll be a big help while we're starving to death and dying of thirst."

"It's always good to see you, troop," said Jane. "But, as Sister says, there are lots of other wonderful merit badges to try for."

"Yeah. The Basket-weaving Badge," grumped Brother.

"Or the Mapmaking Badge," groused Fred.

"Or the Flower-pressing Badge," grumbled Lizzy.

"Well, those are a lot better than starving to death and dying of thirst in some stupid haunted forest!" said Sister.

"Now, please, group," said Jane. "I've got some test papers to mark. So scoot!" Besides being a scout leader, Jane was a teacher at Bear Country School.

The scouts scooted.

• Chapter 2 •

Running into Ralph

The scouts had left Jane's and were walking along her tree-lined street. Fred, Lizzy, and Sister were walking slowly. They were relaxed about Jane's turndown. Not Brother. Hands in pockets, brow knit, he was forging ahead.

"Hey!" called Fred. "Wait up! Where are you going in such a hurry?" Fred and the others had to run to catch up.

"To the library," said Brother.

"The library?" said Fred. "Hey, I'm supposed to be the bookworm in this group, so going to the library's fine with me. But I have to ask a question: Why are we going to the library right now?"

"Because," said Brother, "that's where we can find out how to survive in the wilderness."

"Then you haven't given up on the Wilderness Badge," said Fred.

"Nope," said Brother.

"Sounds kinda tough," said Fred. "I mean, no food and water."

"Just the clothes on your back, a sleeping bag, an ax, and a collapsible cup," said Lizzy.

"Not to mention ghosts," said Sister.

"Sounds *awful* tough," said Fred.

"Sure it sounds tough," said Brother. "But other scouts have earned it, and so can we."

"Maybe we should go see Actual Factual about it," said Lizzy.

"No," said Brother. "Jane was right about that. We can't go running to the professor every time we have a merit-badge problem. He's an important scientist. He has a big museum to run."

The Beartown Library was in the line of important buildings that ringed the little park at the center of town. There was the mayor's office, town hall, the police and fire stations, and Judge Gavel's courthouse. The Bear Scouts were about to cut across the little park and head for the library when they saw a familiar sight: Ralph Ripoff being hassled by Police Chief Bruno.

Ralph was a pickpocket and second-story bear turned swindler. He was a dealer in phony termite insurance, driveway blacktop that never dried, and gold watches that turned green overnight. He had a two-headed coin, cards up his sleeve, and hands that were quicker than the eye. Ralph had cheated just about everybody in town at least once. Folks were pretty angry about it. There were rumors that a citizens' committee was getting organized and planning "to do something about Ralph."

The Bear Scouts knew Ralph well. He lived in a broken-down old houseboat that was moored in a quiet backwater of Great Roaring River. It was the Bear Scouts who had foiled some of Ralph's rottenest schemes. The trouble was that in spite of his low character and wicked ways, the scouts sort of liked him. He was funny and quick, and he wore great clothes: a green plaid suit, a yellow straw hat, and little foot things called spats. He carried a handsome bamboo cane that some said concealed a sword. The scouts had never seen the sword and didn't quite believe it.

"What do you suppose is going on between Ralph and the chief?" said Sister.

"Don't know," said Fred. "But you'd think Ralph would have enough sense not to come so close to the police station. Just seeing Ralph sets Chief Bruno off like a pinwheel."

The chief wasn't exactly pinwheeling, but he was pretty excited about something. Ralph was carrying a strange-looking object. It was covered with a cloth. Chief Bruno was demanding to know what it was and where Ralph got it.

"Let me answer your questions in reverse order, Chief," said Ralph, lifting the cloth. "I got it in the grand salon of my

houseboat, and what it is, as you can
plainly see, is my pet parrot, Squawk."

Sure enough, it was Ralph's pet parrot.
He was sitting on the little swing in his
regular cage. The usually noisy Squawk
was strangely quiet.

"Oh?" said the chief, taken aback. "Well,

tell me this. What are you doing walking around town with a parrot?"

"If, sir, you'll note the shingle on the door next to the police station. It says, 'DR. WORMSER, VETERINARIAN.' It happens that my friend Squawk is ill and we have an appointment with the good doctor."

"Well," grumped Chief Bruno, "just see that you don't get into any trouble!"

"Trouble, indeed, sir," said Ralph. "I've half a mind to step into Judge Gavel's court and charge you with police brutality and cruelty to parrots."

Chief Bruno growled and gritted his teeth as he retreated into the police station.

"Hey, Ralph," said Brother. "You really shouldn't rag the chief that way. He can't handle it."

"Well, well!" said Ralph. "If it isn't my dear little friends the Bear Scouts."

• Chapter 3 •
On to the Library!

The scouts liked Ralph in spite of himself, but they liked Squawk for his own sake. He was a jolly, noisy, boastful little bird who could talk a blue streak. But not today. He was as silent as he was sad-looking.

Ralph set the cage on the ground. The scouts gathered round for a close look.

"Hi there, sweetie!" said Lizzy, who could charm the birds out of the trees.

But she wasn't charming a word out of Squawk. He just sat on his swing, hunched over and silent.

"What's the matter with him, Ralph?" said Brother.

"Laryngitis," said Ralph.

"Laryn-whosis?" said Sister.

As usual, Fred was ready with a definition. "*Laryngitis,*" he said. "*Pronounced lar-in-GI-tis. A soreness of the vocal chords, sometimes causing loss of voice.*"

Squawk opened his beak as if to speak, but he couldn't make a sound.

"Poor little fellow," said Ralph. "It just

breaks my heart to see him like this." He placed the cloth on the cage. "I don't know what I'd do without him. Well," he said with a sigh, "Dr. Wormser awaits."

Ralph picked up the cage with one hand and brushed his eye with the other. Was that a tear Ralph was brushing away? That's the way it was with Ralph. Robbing widows and orphans one minute and all broken up about his sick parrot the next.

"I certainly hope he doesn't have to get a shot," said Ralph. "He's terrified of needles."

The Bear Scouts could understand that. They were a little scared of needles themselves.

"That Ralph," said Fred, shaking his head. "A rotten, low-down, scheming crook, and here he is worried sick about his parrot."

"Yeah," said Sister. "Brought him all the way into town to see the vet."

"You know what my dad says," said Lizzy. "If Ralph went straight and worked as hard at some honest job as he does at thinking up crooked schemes, he could be one of Beartown's leading citizens."

"Instead of its leading crook," said Sister.

"Hey, guys, never mind about Ralph and his parrot," said Brother. "On to the library! We've got a wilderness to survive!"

The scouts followed Brother into the library.

• Chapter 4 •

The Revenge of the Card Catalogue

Mrs. Hushmeyer, the head librarian, greeted the scouts in her usual friendly manner. She knew Fred best, of course. But she knew all the scouts, and since she did the checking out she knew what sort of books they liked. Brother was into mysteries and sports. Sister liked stories about castles and princesses. Lizzy specialized in books about nature. Fred was all over the lot when it came to books. He read everything from science and history to the plays of William Shakesbear — and the dictionary and encyclopedia, of course.

So Mrs. Hushmeyer was surprised when they didn't head straight for their favorite shelves. Instead, they made a beeline for the card catalogue. Hmm, she thought.

"What should we look under?" said Brother.

"I'd say either 'Nature Study' or 'Natural History,'" advised Fred.

They pulled out the N to P drawer. They found the Nature Study section and began looking through the cards. Each card stood for a book. It told the title, the name of the author, the number of pages, and where to find it on the shelves.

"Hey, there's tons of cards under 'Nature Study,'" said Brother.

"Try looking for 'Survival' under 'Nature Study,'" said Fred.

"Way to go, Fred!" shouted Brother. "There's a whole pack of them!"

Brother's shout echoed through the library.

"Hush, please!" said Mrs. Hushmeyer.

"Sorry," said Brother in a much softer voice. "I kinda got carried away. Look, here's just what we're looking for."

Fred leaned in and read the card.
" '*Surviving in the Wilderness* by Forrest Woodside, 792 pages.' That'll be perfect! Come on! It's in section A-7."

But all they found was a 792-page-thick empty place.

"It must be out," said Brother.

"Hey," said Fred. "That's what libraries are for: taking books out. Not to worry. There's lots of other survival titles."

They went back to the card catalogue.

"Here's a good one," said Fred. " '*Stalking the Wild Onion: Finding Food in the Forest* by J.P. Bloodroot.' "

But that book was also among the missing. Other interesting titles were *Catching Fish Without Line or Hook*, *Creating Shelters with Leaf and Bough*, and *The Complete Fungus Finder: How to Tell the Mushrooms from the Toadstools*. But they were all out! Each and every one!

"Well, there goes my big plan," said Brother.

"What plan was that?" said Fred.

"Isn't it obvious?" said Brother. "I was going to bone up on survival methods. I was going to learn so much about catching fish without line or hook, stalking the wild onion, and finding fungus that Scout Leader Jane would *have* to let us try for the Wilderness Survival Merit Badge."

Brother sighed. "Well," he said, "so much for if-at-first-you-don't-succeed."

Mrs. Hushmeyer had been watching the scouts. She was proud of her collection and concerned that they hadn't been able to find what they were looking for.

"Perhaps I can help," said Mrs. Hushmeyer as the scouts passed the checkout counter.

The scouts looked very disappointed — even Sister, who had decided to stand up to her fears about ghosts and join in the excitement of trying for the Wilderness Badge.

"Thanks, Mrs. Hushmeyer," said Brother. "It's just that we wanted to study up on something for a merit badge and every book on the subject is out."

"That's unusual," said Mrs. Hushmeyer. "Do you remember the titles?"

"Sure," said Fred. *"Surviving in the Wilderness, Catching Fish Without Line or Hook, Stalking the Wild Onion . . ."*

"Oh, yes," said Mrs. Hushmeyer. "I remember them well because they were all taken out by the same person."

"Do you mind telling us who that person was?" said Brother.

"Not at all," said Mrs. Hushmeyer. "It was Professor Actual Factual."

"Professor Actual Factual?" said the scouts.

"Yes. He said he was about to go on some sort of survival expedition into the Great Grizzly Forest. I found that very —"

But Mrs. Hushmeyer never got to finish her sentence. The Bear Scouts were out the door in a cloud of dust and headed for the Bearsonian Institution at a shocking rate of speed.

• Chapter 5 •

"Splendid!" Said the Professor

The Bear Scouts got to the Bearsonian in
record time. But they might as well have
walked because they were so out of breath
when they got there that they couldn't
speak.

"Easy, now," said the professor. "Don't try to talk. Take deep breaths. Here, try some sips of water." He gave them each a cup of water. "That's it. Breathe in. Breathe out. I'm sure you've got something very exciting to tell me. There'll be time enough to tell me about it when you've caught your breath."

But the scouts were already trying to tell him about it. First Brother, then the others, saw the pile of survival books on the professor's desk. They began pointing wildly at them.

"Those? They're library books," said the professor. "I took them out a couple of days ago. That thick one is by Professor Woodside over at the university. Terrific chap. Bear Country's greatest expert on living off the land. You know — catching fish without proper gear, finding yummies in the forest. That sort of thing. I'm planning a research trip into Great Grizzly Forest.

Thought I'd do the survival bit at the same time."

That's when the professor noticed that the Bear Scouts had not only caught their breath, they were grinning broadly.

"That's why we're here, professor," said Brother. "We want to go with you!"

It didn't take long for the scouts to tell the professor about their problem with the Wilderness Badge and going to the library and finding that he, Professor Actual Factual, had all the survival books out.

"So what do you say, professor?" said Fred.

"I say splendid!" said Actual Factual. "I shall be delighted to have you with me in the wilderness. I'm very excited about going into the forest primeval, where no bear has gone before. I can't wait to taste one of those gummy bugs. Professor Woodside says they taste rather like chocolate asparagus." The professor didn't

I CAN'T WAIT TO TASTE ONE OF THOSE GUMMY BUGS.

notice, but four scouts swallowed hard at the mention of eating bugs. "You'll need an okay from Scout Leader Jane, of course. And permission from your parents. But I think those things can be worked out."

"Professor," said Fred, "when will you be returning those books? We'd like to check them out when you're finished with them."

"I'm finished with them now," said the professor. "Why don't you take them with you? I'm sure I can clear it with Mrs. Hushmeyer."

"Terrific!" said Fred. "Lizzy and I are

sleeping over at Brother and Sister's tonight. We can bone up and quiz each other."

"One other thing, professor," said Brother. "Have you thought about how you're going to get across Great Roaring River?"

"Yes. I've given that problem a great deal of thought," said the professor. "And I believe I have that worked out. As a matter of fact, I'm going to check out crossing sites tomorrow morning. Why don't you meet me on the riverbank just south of Farmer Ben's farm?"

"It's a date!" said Brother.

The Bear Scouts loaded up on the survival books and headed home.

• Chapter 6 •
Pajama Party Cram Session

The Bear Scouts were in their pajamas and ready for their sleepover. They had enjoyed one of Mama's super suppers of honey-cured salmon and french-fried honeycomb. Now they were in the upstairs playroom in the middle of what turned out to be a combination pajama party and survival cram session.

"This *Stalking the Wild Onion* book is great," said Brother. "There's all kinds of stuff to eat in the forest."

"Besides bugs, I hope," said Lizzy.

Fred had the big thick book. "Here's a

chapter called 'Catching Fish Without Proper Gear,' " he said. He read aloud. " 'We have already discussed the first wilderness survival rule, which is *find water*. The second rule is *find food*. While plant food is plentiful in the form of berries, nuts, roots, and certain kinds of soft inner bark, quality protein is not so easy to obtain. Especially for those unwilling to partake of the many excellent insect foodstuffs found in the forest . . .' "

A good "Yuck!" was had by all. Fred continued.

" '. . . Which brings us to fish. There are many common vines that can be made to serve as a survival fishing line. These include arrow vine, sinew vine, and clawfoot vine. The best hook for your survival line is the thorn of the zigzag bush. Once it is tied to the line with a granny knot, the wilderness survivor is ready to dig for worms.' "

"Or you could just eat the worms in the first place," said Sister. The rest of the troop ignored her.

The scouts were all eyes and ears as Fred leafed ahead in the big survival book. "Here's a whole section on how to make a survival shelter," said Fred. There were how-to pictures on every page. They showed how to build shelters with tree branches and leaves.

"I like how the leaves are laid on like roof shingles," said Lizzy.

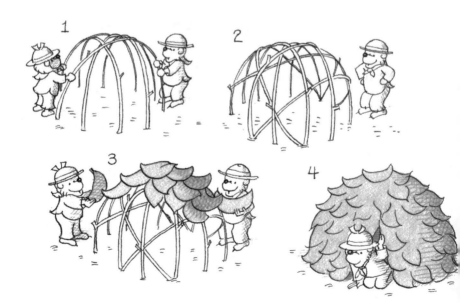

"That's to keep the rain out," said Fred.

As the scouts continued to look through the books, two things happened. They began to understand Scout Leader Jane's concern. Wilderness survival was a serious business. But the more they learned about it, the more they wanted to meet the challenge of trying for the Wilderness Survival Merit Badge. Brother had been gung ho from the beginning. But now the others were excited about it, too — even Sister. There was no more talk about basket weaving, mapmaking, flower pressing — or ghosts.

It was getting late. The pajama party cram session was beginning to wind down. Lizzy was the first one to get the yawns. Soon all the scouts were yawning and stretching. It was time to turn in. The plan was for Brother and Fred to double up in the cubs' room and for Sister and Lizzy to sleep on the daybed in the playroom.

While Brother and Fred were busy yawning and stretching, Sister and Lizzy grabbed first turn in the bathroom. They left the playroom and headed down the hall. But they were back in a shot.

"Hey, you two," said Lizzy. "Did you know there's some kind of meeting going on downstairs?"

"Meeting? Downstairs?" said Brother.

"Yes," said Sister. "And it seems to have something to do with Ralph."

"Who's down there?" said Brother.

"Your mom and dad," said Lizzy. "My mom and dad, Fred's, Farmer and Mrs. Ben, Gramps and Gran, Widder McGrizz, Dr. Gert, and a couple others."

"Why do you suppose they're having a meeting about Ralph?" said Brother.

"Is there anything in the Bear Scout Oath against eavesdropping?" said Sister.

"Nope," said Fred.

"Then let's eavesdrop," said Sister.

• Chapter 7 •

What the Bear Scouts Overheard

The scouts turned out the upstairs lights.
They tiptoed down the hall and sat on the
steps. It was dark at the top of the stairs.
But, down below, the living room was
ablaze with light and fiery speeches. The
scouts couldn't hear exactly what was being said because everyone was talking at
once. But one thing was clear. The meeting
wasn't about giving Ralph a good conduct
medal; it was about running him out of
town.

There was a knocking sound. It was
Gramps rapping his pocket watch on a

table. "Order!" he shouted. "Let's bring this citizens' committee meeting to order! We're not going to do anything about that no-good scalawag if we just sit here cackling like crows in a cornfield. Farmer Ben, you seem to be the angriest. You have the floor."

"Darn right I'm angry. Got a right to be. Why, some of the schemes he's pulled on me and my missus would make your fur curl. Sold me some odorless fertilizer. Killed half my sweet peas. Sold me some cow vitamins. Milk came out purple."

"Well, what are we gonna do about it?" cried Papa.

"It's time for action!" shouted Fred's dad.

"I say tar and feather him and run him out of town on a rail!" cried Lizzy's dad.

"A splintery rail!" added Farmer Ben. "And while we're at it, let's sink that dang houseboat of his. We'll just put a hole in its bottom and it'll be glub, glub, good-bye, houseboat!"

There were shouts of agreement. "Right!" "Let's go get him!" "I'll bring the

tar!" "I'll bring the feathers!" "I'll bring the rail!"

The Bear Scouts sat at the top of the stairs hugging their knees. There was a lot of anger in that room. It was rising off the crowd like steam off a hot highway. It was a little frightening.

Gramps was banging his watch on the table again. "Order! Order!" shouted Gramps. "The chair joins in your ideas. Therefore, be it resolved: It is the sense of the citizens' committee that one Ralph Ripoff be dealt with as follows: His filthy houseboat is to be sunk, and he is to be tarred and feathered and run out of town on a splintery rail. All those in favor, say 'Aye!'"

But before the *ayes* could have it, a voice cut the air.

"Hold everything!" It was Gran. "I haven't said anything up to now. But the time has come for me to have my say —

and here it is. We all know that there's no fool like an old fool." She looked hard at Gramps. "But there's a much worse kind of foolishness. That's the foolishness of a mob. And that's what you're turning into, a mob that's gonna take the law into its own hands!"

"Gran's right," said Mama. "You're right to be upset with Ralph. There's no doubt that Ralph's schemes come close to being crooked. But that's a matter for the police."

"That's the problem!" said Papa. "Ralph *comes close* to breaking the law. But he never quite crosses the line."

As with most arguments, there were two sides to the one about Ralph. Soon everybody was talking at once again. But more quietly this time. There was still a lot of anger against Ralph. But some of the steam had gone out of it.

"All right," said Gramps, taking charge again. "We'll table the motion to tar and feather Ralph, sink his houseboat, and run him out of town on a splintery rail. All those in favor of tabling, say 'Aye!' "

The *ayes* had it, Farmer Ben being the only holdout.

"But!" added Gramps. "If Ralph pulls one more crooked scheme, sells one more phony gold watch, pulls one more ace out of his sleeve, we start gathering feathers and cooking tar. All those in favor of that, say 'Aye.' "

This time there were no holdouts.

"Now, friends," said Gramps, "this

meeting of the citizens' committee is adjourned so we can enjoy the molasses cookies and sassafras tea that Mama has just served."

The scouts had heard enough. They certainly could understand that folks didn't like being cheated and robbed. After all, it was the scouts themselves who had fought Ralph to a standstill and foiled some of his worst schemes.

What was it the citizens' committee had decided? They would give Ralph one more chance. *Then* they would go after him with tar and feathers and sink his houseboat.

Maybe they should warn Ralph. Tell him about the danger he faced. Maybe Ralph could be "scared straight." It was a long shot. But maybe, just maybe . . .

Such were the thoughts of the Bear Scouts as they drifted off to sleep.

• Chapter 8 •

A Warning for Ralph

When the Bear Scouts met the professor
on the bank of Great Roaring River the
next morning, they told him about the citizens' committee meeting.

"Oh, dear," said the professor. "I don't
like the sound of that at all. You say they
passed some sort of ruling. Do you remember what it said?"

"I remember exactly," said Brother. "It
said that if Ralph pulled one more crooked
scheme, sold one more phony gold watch,
pulled one more ace out of his sleeve, they
would tar and feather him, sink his house-

boat, and run him out of town on a splintery rail."

"That does sound serious," said the professor. "And it's your idea to warn him in order to frighten him into becoming an honest citizen?"

"Right," said Brother. "We're going to try to scare him straight."

"Do you think it'll work, professor?" said Fred.

"I don't know," said the professor. "But I don't see what harm it can do. Getting Mr. Ripoff to change his ways would be a great boon to bearkind. I think you should give it a try. We'll stop off at Mr. Ripoff's on our way upriver."

The scouts hadn't been by Ralph's house for some time. While Ralph's home afloat had never been a candidate for the cover of *Houseboat Beautiful*, it was clear, as it came into view, that it had gone from bad to worse. The weeds on the bank had

grown so tall that all that showed of
Ralph's mailbox was the little red flag.

Ralph's Place was moored in a quiet
backwater away from the powerful cur-
rents of Great Roaring River. It was green
with mold and spotted with rot. The
brightwork needed lots of brass polish and
even more elbow grease. Dragonflies
hummed and hovered. The green scum,
which lay thick on the water, had begun to
creep up the gangplank.

"Hello, the houseboat!" called Brother. "Permission to come aboard!"

Ralph appeared at the head of the gangplank. "Well, bless my spats if it isn't my Bear Scout friends! Permission granted!"

"You know Professor Actual Factual," said Brother as they climbed aboard.

"The whole world knows the foremost bear scientist of his time," said Ralph. "I'm honored, sir. I've cased — er, visited — your magnificent museum many times. I especially admire your collection of gems and precious metals."

"I'll bet," whispered Sister.

"Why, thank you, Mr. Ripoff. That's very kind of you."

"You are here to ask after the health of Squawk, my pet parrot, no doubt," said Ralph. "I'm happy to tell you he's much better. Come in and have a look."

The Bear Scouts and the professor followed Ralph into the main cabin.

"This is the grand salon," said Ralph.

"Grand mess is more like it," said Sister under her breath.

Ralph's Place was indeed a mess. There were half-eaten snacks all over, spiderwebs in the corners, and dust devils under the furniture.

"And there," said Ralph, "is my great and good friend Squawk, restored to good health."

"Welcome aboard! Welcome aboard!" squawked Squawk. "Take a card! Any card at all!"

"He's certainly got his voice back," said Lizzy.

"We're glad Squawk is well," said Brother. "But that's not exactly why we're here."

"What *are* you doing in this neck of the woods?" said Ralph.

"Actually," said Actual Factual, "we're planning an expedition into Great Grizzly Forest, and we're checking out the river for a crossing site."

"You can't be serious!" said Ralph.

"I assure you, sir, we're quite serious," said the professor. "I'm going to do some research, and the scouts are going to try for the Wilderness Survival Merit Badge."

"Don't do it!" said Ralph. "Don't even *think* about it!"

"Why ever not?" said Actual Factual.

"Because," said Ralph, "Great Grizzly Forest is *haunted*. It's safe enough by day.

But at night all manner of ghosts, spooks, and freaks race through the forest screaming and wailing. And not just plain vanilla ghosts. There are free-floating heads, grasping hands, glowing eyeballs!"

The scouts couldn't tell whether Ralph was serious or not. He did have a teasing twinkle in his eye. But that didn't prove anything. Ralph always had that twinkle in his eye.

"Survival Merit Badge, huh?" said Ralph with a chuckle. "You won't survive in that forest a single night. You'll come screaming out of there by nightfall. *If you're lucky!*"

"Oh yeah?" said Fred.

"Wanna bet?" said Brother.

"There's no such thing as ghosts!" said Lizzy.

"Th-th-that's right," said Sister. "You c-c-can't scare us."

"With all respect, sir," said the professor, "I am a bear of science. And while I admit that nothing is truly impossible, I must tell you that I regard your warning about ghosts as pure mischief-making nonsense. Now, if you'll excuse us, sir, we have a crossing site to select."

"Wait, professor," said Brother. "Speaking of warnings, let's not forget why we're here: to warn Ralph."

"About what?" said Ralph.

"About the citizens' committee," said Brother.

That got Ralph's attention. "Citizens' committee, huh?" said Ralph. "I don't like the sound of that. When I hear the words 'citizens' committee,' I reach for my sword

cane." Suddenly, Ralph was on his feet, leaping about the cabin, thrusting and parrying with his cane.

"Ralph," said Sister. "Do you really have a sword in that cane?"

"That, little girl," said Ralph, "is for me to know and for you to find out. Tell me more about this citizens' committee," Ralph said, putting aside his cane.

"Well," said Brother, "there's not all that much to tell. It's just that certain citizens are pretty angry about all the crooked schemes you've pulled."

"And . . ." said Ralph.

"And if you pull one more crooked scheme," continued Brother, "they're gonna tar and feather you, sink your houseboat, and run you out of town on a splintery rail."

That *really* got Ralph's attention.

• Chapter 9 •

A Bargain with Ralph

Ralph was silent for a long moment. "Tell me something," he said. "Why are you telling me this? Why are you warning me about what this so-called citizens' committee is going to do to me?"

"Because," said Brother. "Well, let's put it this way: Have you ever thought about turning honest, not being a crook?"

"You mean . . . go *straight*?" The very word was like castor oil in Ralph's mouth. "You don't know what you're asking. It would mean giving up the career of a lifetime. Why would I do a thing like that? What would be in it for me?"

"It would get the citizens' committee off your back," said Brother.

"It would cancel out the tar and feathers," said Fred.

"And the sunken houseboat," said Lizzy.

"And the splintery rail," said Sister.

"Look," said Ralph. "If I worried about the likes of citizens' committees, I'd have gone straight years ago. No, there's got to be more in it than that."

The scouts sensed that Ralph was more worried about the committee than he was letting on. They pressed their case.

"Like what?" said Brother.

"Remember a little while ago when I said you wouldn't stay in Great Grizzly Forest a whole night and you said, 'Wanna bet?'"

"I remember," said Brother.

"Well, I happen to be a betting bear,"

said Ralph. "So, let's make things more interesting with a little wager. Try this on for size: I, Ralph Ripoff, bet that if you, the Bear Scouts, can stay in Great Grizzly Forest for one whole night, I will go straight."

"You mean no more crooked schemes, no more phony gold watches, no more cards up your sleeve?" said Brother.

"Exactly," said Ralph.

"Ralph, you've got a bet!" said Brother.

"Just a minute," said Ralph. "Don't you want to hear the other side of the bet?"

"There's no chance we're going to get scared out of the forest," said Brother. "But I suppose we ought to know the other side of the bet."

"Here it is," said Ralph. "If you, the Bear Scouts, *fail* to stay in the forest for one whole night, then you must take care of this houseboat for one year. You must cut the weeds, polish the brass, and keep it neat and clean inside and out."

The scouts looked around. The house-boat certainly was a mess. But they didn't hesitate. They thrust out their hands and said, "It's a bet."

Ralph took their small hands in his large ones. "My friends," he said with a big smile, "it's been a pleasure doing business with you."

After Ralph let the Bear Scouts and the professor out, he turned to Squawk. "Like taking candy from a baby," he said.

"Candy from a baby! Candy from a baby! Candy from a baby!" squawked Squawk.

• Chapter 10 •

Smelling a Rat

Scout Leader Jane was a little testy the
second time around. She quizzed the
scouts hard on how they managed to bring
Professor Actual Factual in on the Wilderness Survival Merit Badge.

"It happened just the way we told you,"
said Brother. "Actual Factual was already
planning a trip into Great Grizzly Forest.
Scout's honor."

Jane knew that a straight arrow like
Brother would never claim scout's honor
without good reason.

Jane quizzed the scouts even harder on survival methods. She had a long list of questions. She quizzed them on finding water, finding food, building a shelter, building a fire, and many other survival subjects. But the Bear Scouts had studied hard and answered every question correctly.

"I'm impressed," said Jane. "You've really done your homework. So, you have my go-ahead on trying for the Wilderness Survival Merit Badge. But please understand, without Professor Actual Factual, there would have been no chance. Meanwhile, have you gotten your parents' permission yet?"

"Yes," said Fred. "They finally gave in when they heard that Actual Factual was taking a two-way police radio along."

"You know," said Lizzy. "In case of an emergency."

"Not to mention ghosts," said Sister.

In fact, Actual Factual was pulling into the police parking lot at that very moment. Chief Bruno had insisted that Actual Factual take a police radio along on an expedition that might be dangerous. And while the professor thought the chief was something of a worrywart, he appreciated his interest and concern.

The professor was just about to go into the police station to pick up the radio when he saw something that was too interesting to ignore. He saw Ralph Ripoff coming out of a store carrying a large box. The store was on a narrow side street. Actual Factual couldn't remember what kind of store it was. He decided to investigate, and he headed up the side street.

It wasn't until he was standing in front of its display window that he remembered the store. It was Beartown Theatrical Supply: Costumes and Masks a Specialty. A number of costumes and masks were on display. Two were of the fancy-dress variety. One was a Spanish dancer's costume. It had a shiny black wig with red combs, a silk dress, and shoes with silver buckles. The other was a royal princess's costume with a tiara, a scepter, and a flowing robe.

But most of the costumes and masks on display were scary. There was a rack of rubber masks. On it were a Frankenbear with a bolt through its neck, a vampire with red fangs, and a drooling maniac monster.

But the scariest thing in the window was a huge ghost costume. And it wasn't plain vanilla. It had bloodshot eyes, a droop snoot, and an ugly blood-smeared mouth. Just looking at it gave Actual Factual the shivers. The professor was beginning to smell a rat, a rat named Ralph Ripoff.

An old-fashioned over-the-door bell rang as Actual Factual entered the store.

The storekeeper was behind a counter. The walls were stacked with costume boxes marked "PIRATE," "BALLERINA," "ADMIRAL OF THE SEAS," and the like.

"May I help you, sir?" said the storekeeper.

"Why, yes. I think perhaps you can," said the professor. "I just saw a friend of mine leave your store with a box. Could you tell me what costume he chose? You see, we're going to the same costume ball and it wouldn't do for me to wear the same costume."

"I couldn't tell you that, sir," said the storekeeper. "That would be giving away his secret. But I can do this. You tell me what sort of costume you have in mind, and if there's any conflict . . ."

"Oh, I was thinking of a pirate costume," said the professor. "Or perhaps an admiral of the seas costume."

"You'll be safe with either of those, sir. Your friend's costume was, shall we say, of the scary variety. Now, if you'll just step over . . . wait, sir! Where are you going?"

"I'll be back when I've made up my mind," said the professor.

He went directly to the police station and picked up the two-way radio. It was starting to get dark. They would be crossing the river to Great Grizzly Forest first thing in the morning, so there wasn't much time.

It was dark by the time he got back to the Bearsonian. He made his way through the darkened museum to the Hall of Culture. He went to the section on witchcraft and witchdoctory. He put on the light and looked around. What he saw was even scarier than Beartown Theatrical Supply: Costumes and Masks a Specialty.

• Chapter 11 •

Crossing the River

When the Bear Scouts arrived at the Bearsonian the next morning, they were all set for their move into the forest primeval. They went around to the parking lot where Actual Factual was loading the sciencemobile.

The scouts were traveling light. Each scout had one Bear Scout uniform (which they were wearing, of course), one Bear Scout sleeping bag, one Bear Scout ax, and one collapsible metal cup. The professor, who was not bound by Bear Scout rules, was loading gear into the sciencemobile.

"Professor," said Brother, "isn't that an awful lot of gear for a *survival* trip?"

"You forget," said Actual Factual, "that for me this is a research trip. This is mostly research gear: vials, test tubes, a camera, extra film, litmus paper — that sort of thing."

The scouts didn't think about it at the time. But if they had, they might have wondered why a few research items made such a large package.

"Actually," said Actual Factual, "when it comes to survival, I'm going to follow exactly the same rules as you scouts."

"What's that thing?" said Lizzy.

The professor was loading a strange-looking object that looked like a cross between a cookpot and a small cannon. The pot was filled with coiled rope, and the cannon had what looked like a bunch of giant fish hooks in its mouth. It was so strange-looking that the scouts couldn't help wondering what it could possibly have to do with surviving in the wilderness. As it turned out, it didn't have anything to do with surviving in the wilderness. It had to do with *getting* there.

Great Roaring River came by its name honestly. It was great, and it roared — so loudly that Actual Factual had to gather the scouts to make himself heard. And even then he had to shout.

"You were wondering how we were going to get across the river," shouted the professor. "Well, this is how. It's my latest invention. It's called a grappling gun." He set the thing on the bank. "All right. Now, stand back and cover your ears." Then he stretched on his belly, reached out, and pressed a button.

The roar of the river was nothing compared to the roar of the gun. There was an enormous *BLAM!* The explosion sent the grappling hooks and their tail of rope clear across the river and into the trees on the other side.

"Now, pull!" shouted the professor.

The scouts pulled. Actual Factual wound the rope around a tree and tied it fast.

"You don't expect us to cross hand over hand on that rope?" said Fred.

"Perish the thought," said the professor, who had already inflated a rubber boat. It had a built-in motor and built-in cables with snap-on hooks.

The professor handed out life jackets and snapped the hooks onto the crossing rope. He loaded the Bear Scouts and his gear into the boat. Then he started the motor, and off they went putt-putting across the Great Roaring River. The Bear Scouts were impressed.

So was someone else who was watching from the bushes. Someone who had his own plans for crossing the river and was grateful to see how it was done. Someone who was hard to see because his green plaid suit blended so well with the bushes.

• Chapter 12 •

The Great Lodgepole
Pine Massacre

After the thrill of crossing the river,
reaching the other side was a letdown.
The trees and bushes on the Great Grizzly
Forest side were the same as those on the
near side.

There was a lot of work to do before
they moved into the forest. First, they had
to climb the steep riverbank. Then, after
deflating the rubber boat, they had to
gather brush to hide the life jackets and
the boat. Next, they helped Actual Factual
organize his gear into a pack and hoist it

onto his back. The professor, who was an experienced trekker, was as fresh as a daisy. But the scouts were already beginning to get tired and thirsty.

But once they moved into the great forest, they forgot about being tired and thirsty. That letdown feeling gave way to a feeling of wonder. They had left the scrub and brush of the riverbank behind. Now they were walking among trees whose trunks were so great that it would have taken all four scouts to give one a hug.

Except for distant birdsong and the sound of their own footsteps, all was silent. The ground was spongy with the leaf fall of years and years of seasons. Actual Factual had taken out a small notebook and was making notes.

"What are you writing down, professor?" said Fred.

"I'm just noting the different kinds of trees," said the professor. "Nothing un-

usual so far. Some ash. Some poplar. But mostly maple and oak. Just about what you'd expect."

Suddenly, the professor froze in his tracks. "Look!" he said. The scouts froze with him.

"It's just a squirrel," said Sister.

"Yes," said the professor. "But it's a red squirrel. Local squirrels are gray. Red squirrels are unusual, even rare, in these parts."

"The professor's right," said Lizzy, some of whose best friends were gray squirrels.

"It's still just a squirrel," said Sister. "Is it important whether it's gray or red?"

"It could be," said Actual Factual. "Sometimes split-off places like this have different flora and fauna."

"Who the heck are Flora and Fauna?" said Sister.

"Definitions, Fred," said the professor.

"Flora," said Fred. "Pronounced *FLAW-ra: plants and plant life of all kinds.* Fauna, pronounced *FAW-na: the full range of animals and animal life.*"

"Thank you, Fred," said the professor. "Red squirrels usually live in or near pine forests. So we should begin seeing pine trees soon."

Which indeed they did. Big black-trunked pine trees began showing up among the maples and oaks.

The professor stopped taking notes and began to walk faster. He was becoming excited about something. Was it the squirrels or the trees? Why would anyone get excited about pine trees?

Finally, Actual Factual stopped at one of the big black-trunked trees. He stood close to it and sighted up its straight trunk as if it were a rifle and he was aiming at the sky. "Amazing!" he said. "I do believe this is a lodgepole pine!"

The scouts looked at each other and shrugged, as if to say, "So it's some kind of pine tree. Big deal." But when they turned to ask Actual Factual to explain, he was off into the forest. He was darting from tree to tree, shouting, "Lodgepole pine! Lodgepole pine! And another! And another!" Soon he was out of sight.

"Come on!" said Brother, in a bit of a panic. "We've got to find him!"

They found him just beyond where they'd seen him last. He was sitting on a stump, making notes.

"Oh, professor," said Brother.

Actual Factual looked up at the scouts

as if he'd forgotten about them. Which, for the moment, he had.

"Ah, yes, the Bear Scouts," he said. "Sorry to have gotten carried away like that. But to find a stand of healthy lodgepole pines is truly amazing!"

Actual Factual read the puzzlement on the scouts' faces. He explained why he was so excited. "At one time, many years ago," he said, "lodgepole pines grew all over Bear Country. Then, one spring, they were attacked by the deadly lodgepole blight. The entire crop was destroyed. It was a great loss. Lodgepole pines were very valuable. They were the tallest, straightest trees in Bear Country. They were used for ship masts, flagpoles, for center poles of circus tents, all sorts of things. So to find a stand of them here in this great forest, where no bear has gone before, is a truly important discovery."

"I have a question, sir," said Sister.

"Yes?" said the professor.

"If this is a forest primeval, where no bear has gone before," said Sister, "who cut down that tree you're sitting on the stump of?"

The professor leaped up as if he'd been sitting on a hot seat. He looked at the stump.

"A most interesting question, my dear," said the professor. He looked closely at its cut surface. He ran his hand over it. "There is no question about it," he said. "This is the stump of a lodgepole pine that was cut down with a chain saw."

Fred and Lizzy had gone off to look for water and were checking out what they thought was a clearing.

"Professor!" cried Fred. "Come quick!"

It was a clearing, all right. A clearing about the size of a Little League field. But it wasn't a field of dreams. It was a field of stumps. The stumps of dozens and dozens of lodgepole pines.

Actual Factual and the scouts looked at the clearing. It was like a lodgepole pine graveyard.

Sister looked around nervously. It was kind of spooky. "Y-y-you know something," she said in a small voice. "M-m-maybe this forest is haunted after all."

"No, my dear," said Actual Factual. "This is not the work of ghosts, spooks, and haunts. This is the work of a criminal gang with chain saws."

• Chapter 13 •

Thirsty, Hungry, and Tired

According to the professor, the great lodgepole pine massacre was the work of a criminal gang so evil that they simply had to be caught and punished. He went right to work gathering evidence. He counted the stumps. He took samples of sawdust. He searched for clues.

"Oh, professor," called Brother, who was waiting with the other scouts at the edge of the clearing. "May we have a word with you?"

"Why, of course," said Actual Factual.

"Professor, we're just as sorry about

those lodgepole pines as you are," said Brother, "but we want to do our Wilderness Survival Merit Badge things. We want to stalk the wild onion, catch fish with a zigzag thorn, make a shelter out of branches and leaves. But mostly, professor, *we're getting really thirsty!*"

"*And hungry!*" said Fred.

Actual Factual hit himself on the side of the head. "How thoughtless of me!" he said. "Please forgive me. I'm a bit of a camel, you see. I've learned to control my thirst on long desert treks. Of course, you want to do your merit-badge things. You shall do them all. There are wild onions all through here. And lots of zigzag bushes. And plenty of material for making a shelter. But first we shall find water. It happens that the chain-saw gang will help us find it. See these tracks?"

There were tire tracks and drag marks leading out of the clearing.

"This is how the gang moved the lodge-pole trunks. But the only way they could have gotten them out of the forest was by floating them on water. So come on!"

They followed the tracks. Soon they came to a large, fast-flowing stream. Stacked on its bank were about a dozen lodgepole trunks.

"Quickly, scouts, fill your cups," said the professor. "Then we'll see about setting up a proper camp."

Sister looked around nervously. She had the feeling they were being watched.

She was right. The forest had more eyes than a potato. They weren't the eyes of ghosts, spooks, and haunts. They were the eyes of the chain-saw gang.

• Chapter 14 •

Wild Onions and Chain-saw Teeth

"We're thirsty," said Sister. "Why can't we just drink the water?"

"Yeah! Why can't we?" said Fred.

"Yeah! We're thirsty!" said Lizzy.

"You can if you want to," said Brother. "But if you do, we won't be able to claim

the Wilderness Survival Badge. Because the merit-badge rules say all water must be boiled before drinking."

"But who will know?" said Sister.

"We'll know," said Brother. "And not only that. We all signed the Bear Scout Oath. And while the oath doesn't say anything about eavesdropping, it's real clear about honesty."

The rest of the troop thought about that. The Bear Scout Oath said, "A scout is as honest as the day is long."

Sister, Fred, and Lizzy sighed. It was going to be a long day indeed if they followed all the Bear Scout rules. But Brother was right. An oath was an oath. And rules were rules.

So they went to work making a Bear Scout fire, using a "fiddle" stick, a green-stick bow, and some dry leaves. It took some doing. But after it was done they were glad they did it. They drank the water while it was still warm. It was the most delicious water they'd ever tasted.

The scouts spent the rest of the day finding food and building a shelter. Finding wild berries was easy and fun, though most berry bushes have thorns. But berry bush thorns were nothing compared to zigzag bush thorns. The scouts managed to catch some fish with them. But they caught many more of their own fingers. *Ouch!*

Wild onions were easy to find. But you couldn't eat them right out of the ground. They were covered with dirt. So the scouts waited until they'd pulled a bunch of them. Then they took turns running them to the stream to be washed.

Building a shelter was a lot harder than it looked in the how-to pictures. But again the scouts managed to get it done.

By the end of the day the scouts were too hungry and tired to think about anything but dinner and climbing into their sleeping bags. The professor had been busy, too. He had taken a flora and fauna census. And he continued to gather evidence about the lodgepole pines. He took photographs of both the stumps and the tire marks. He also found seven broken-off chain-saw teeth.

As evening fell, the Bear Scouts and the professor sat around the campfire and shared a dinner of toasted fish and wild onions, with wild berries for dessert. It had been a long, hard day. Now all the scouts had to do to earn the Wilderness Survival Merit Badge was last through the night.

By nightfall the scouts could hardly keep their eyes open. Brother, Fred, and Lizzy fell fast asleep as soon as they climbed into their sleeping bags. Sister tried to stay awake and watch for ghosts. But she was no more successful than she had been when she had tried to stay awake so she could see Santa Bear.

Actual Factual didn't go to sleep. He was expecting a guest, a ghostly guest for whom he had prepared an interesting welcome.

• Chapter 15 •

Ghost versus Ghost

The brightly burning fire made it difficult to see into the forest. Actual Factual let the fire burn down to glowing embers. Once he was sure the Bear Scouts were sleeping soundly, he went to his supply pack. He dragged it off into the darkness and made ready to welcome the rat he had smelled the day before at Beartown Theatrical Supply.

Hours later something woke Sister. She thought it was the sound of her own snoring. At first she didn't know where she was. But when she saw her sleeping fellow scouts, she not only knew where she was, she knew that it wasn't the sound of her own snoring that woke her. It was a low, wailing sound. A *scary*, low, wailing sound. She looked for Actual Factual. But he wasn't there. It was a sound that started low, then built into wild, cackling laughter.

Great, thought Sister. A ghost with a sense of humor.

She was about to wake her fellow scouts when sight was added to sound. A hideous sight. It was a ghost, all right. A huge, glowing ghost with bloodshot eyes, a droop snoot, and a blood-smeared mouth.

Sister screamed so loud it could easily have scared the ghost. It certainly woke her fellow scouts.

The only thing scarier than ghosts you *do* believe in are ghosts you *don't* believe in. The screams and shouts of the other scouts almost drowned out the wild, wailing, cackling laughter of the droopsnooted, bloodshot, blood-smeared ghost. Where *was* that Actual Factual?

The scouts had struggled out of their sleeping bags and were trying to escape. But it isn't easy to escape into a dark forest. They tripped over roots. They ran into

trees. They got tangled up in zigzag bushes. As the huge, swaying, cackling ghost came after them, it stepped into the glowing embers of the campfire. As it did so, it let out a great "YIPE!"

It's not easy to keep your head while those around you are losing theirs. But Sister kept hers. A thought crossed her mind, a thought followed by an interesting fact. The thought was that a real ghost wouldn't even have felt the fire, much less holler "Yipe!" The interesting fact was that the ghost was wearing spats.

"Don't run away, scouts!" shouted Sister. "This is no ghost! It's that no-good low-down crook, Ralph Ripoff. He's just trying to scare us out of the forest to win the bet!"

But the scouts were no longer running away. Because now it was ghost versus ghost! They were running back toward Sister. They were running away from an even scarier ghost. It was a three-headed *groaning* ghost. It was coming after the scouts and Ralph.

Ralph tripped and fell over backward.

The scouts fell on top of him. The three-headed ghost was almost on them when something stopped it in its tracks. It was a third ghost. So now it was ghost versus ghost versus ghost. This new ghost was a witch doctor ghost. It was the scariest one yet.

As the witch doctor ghost moved for-

ward, the three-headed ghost retreated. Some overhanging branches took hold of its shroud and pulled it off the monster. Beneath the shroud were three creatures who were far more dangerous than any ghost. They were the Bogg brothers, Bear Country's Public Enemies One, Two, and Three! Each was holding a chain saw with some missing teeth.

The Bogg brothers and the chain-saw gang were one and the same!

"Run for your lives!" cried the witch doctor ghost, who was actually Actual Factual, of course.

And everybody did. Everybody, that is, except a certain former ghost named Ralph Ripoff. He did the bravest thing that the professor and the Bear Scouts had ever seen. He stood his ground and bared his cane sword. "En garde!" he shouted. Then, while the Bogg brothers were desperately trying to start their

chain saws, he leaped forward and cut the straps of their old-fashioned single-strap overalls with three quick *snicks*. Of course, their overalls fell around their feet. The Boggs were so embarrassed (they were wearing red long johns) that they dropped their chain saws and tried to pull up their overalls.

At that moment a circle of lights shone on the embarrassed Boggs. Behind the

lights were Chief Bruno and some state troopers he had called in. Actual Factual had called the chief on the two-way radio.

"Hands up!" shouted the chief.

When the Boggs raised their hands, their overalls fell down again.

"Cuff 'em, Officer Marguerite!" said the chief.

"Hey!" complained the head Bogg. "It's cruel and unusual punishment having a lady cop see us in our underwear."

"It's no worse than you deserve," said Chief Bruno.

It was just starting to get light. The Bear Scouts had managed to last through the night. They couldn't help being pleased with themselves. They had not only earned the Wilderness Survival Merit Badge, they had won their bet with Ralph Ripoff, crook, swindler, ghost — and hero.

• Chapter 16 •

Ralph Ripoff, Hero

The Bear Scouts and the professor were mentioned in the newspaper stories about the events that took place in Great Grizzly Forest. But it was Ralph who got the headlines:

★ BEARTOWN GAZZETTE ★
LOCAL CITIZEN RALPH RIPOFF
PROVES HERO IN CAPTURE
OF BOGG BROTHERS:

·THE BEAR TIMES
CRIMEFIGHTER
RALPH RIPOFF CAPTURES
CRIMINAL GANG
HERO: ...CLAREDE

··BEAR COUNTRY NEWS··
RALPH RIPOFF, LOCAL
BEAR-ABOUT-TOWN, FOILS
CRIMINAL GANG

Professor Actual Factual, the Bear Scouts, and Chief Bruno all appeared at the trial. But it was Ralph who was the star witness against the Bogg brothers. They were convicted after a short trial. After all, they were caught red-handed (and red-underweared), and there was strong evidence against them. The broken-off chain-saw teeth were a perfect fit for the Boggs' chain saws.

While the scouts had won the bet, Ralph, as a big hero, was having no trouble going straight (at least for a while). It was Chief Bruno who was having a hard time. He was so used to dealing with Ralph the crook that he didn't quite know how to deal with Ralph the hero.

The citizens' committee had a problem, too. Especially when Ralph, as a citizen and hero in good standing, applied for membership. The question was whether to accept Ralph or disband. They decided to disband.

The way things worked out, Ralph may as well have won the bet. After the excitement died down, the scouts decided to stop by Ralph's houseboat and thank him for saving them from the three-headed ghost. When they got there, they were surprised to see him hard at work cleaning his houseboat. The scouts wondered why.

Ralph showed them a telegram. It was from *Houseboat Beautiful*. It said, "Dear Mr. Ripoff — we, the editors, wish to put your houseboat, Ralph's Place, on the cover of our magazine." It was signed, "The Editors."

The scouts had a quick meeting. What better way, they decided, to thank Ralph for his heroism than to pitch in and help him prepare his houseboat for the cover of *Houseboat Beautiful*.

It took two full days of scrubbing, scraping, sweeping, and polishing. But the

job got done. Ralph showed his apprecia-
tion by asking the scouts to pose with him
in front of the houseboat for the cover
picture.

• About the Authors •

Stan and Jan Berenstain have been writing and illustrating books about bears for more than thirty years. Their very first book about the Bear Scout characters was published in 1967. Through the years the Bear Scouts have done their best to defend the weak, catch the crooked, joust against the unjust, and rally against rottenness of all kinds. In fact, the scouts have done such a great job of living up to the Bear Scout Oath, the authors say, that "they deserve a series of their own."

Stan and Jan Berenstain live in Bucks County, Pennsylvania. They have two sons, Michael and Leo, and four grandchildren. Michael is an artist, and Leo is a writer. Michael did the pictures in this book.

Don't Miss
THE Berenstain BEAR SCOUTS
and the Sinister Smoke Ring

Fred and Lizzy were waiting the next morning on Eagle Road. Sister showed up at nine o'clock sharp.

"I've got bad news, worse news, and worst news," said Sister. "The bad news is that Brother's definitely been hanging out with Too-Tall."

"How do you know?" asked Fred.

"It's obvious," said Sister. "He's been acting more and more like Too-Tall for a couple of days. You know, talking out of the side of his mouth, acting tough, throwing his weight around. And last night I caught him practising Too-Tall poses in front of the mirror. It's a clear case of hero worship."

Fred and Lizzy looked glum. "Okay, what's the worse news?" asked Lizzy.

"The worse news is that he's not only hanging out with the Too-Tall gang, he's smoking with them."

"Hoo-ee!" said Lizzy.

"Guh!" said Fred.

The both looked as if they'd been punched in the belly. Acting tough was one thing. Hanging out was another. But smoking was a whole different thing.

THE Berenstain BEAR® SCOUTS

by Stan & Jan Berenstain

Join Scouts Brother, Sister, Fred, and Lizzy as they defend the weak, catch the crooked, joust against the unjust, and rally against rottenness of all kinds!

☐ BBF60384-1	The Berenstain Bear Scouts and the Coughing Catfish	$2.99
☐ BBF60380-9	The Berenstain Bear Scouts and the Humongous Pumpkin	$2.99
☐ BBF60385-X	The Berenstain Bear Scouts and the Sci-Fi Pizza	$2.99
☐ BBF94473-8	The Berenstain Bear Scouts and the Sinister Smoke Ring	$3.50
☐ BBF60383-3	The Berenstain Bear Scouts and the Terrible Talking Termite	$2.99
☐ BBF60386-8	The Berenstain Bear Scouts Ghost Versus Ghost	$2.99
☐ BBF60379-5	The Berenstain Bear Scouts in Giant Bat Cave	$2.99
☐ BBF60381-7	The Berenstain Bear Scouts Meet Bigpaw	$2.99
☐ BBF60382-5	The Berenstain Bear Scouts Save That Backscratcher	$2.99
☐ BBF94475-4	The Berenstain Bear Scouts and the Magic Crystal Caper	$3.50
☐ BBF94477-0	The Berenstain Bear Scouts and the Run-Amuck Robot	$3.50
☐ BBF94479-7	The Berenstain Bear Scouts and the Ice Monster	$3.50
☐ BBF94481-9	The Berenstain Bear Scouts and the Really Big Disaster	$3.50
☐ BBF94484-3	The Berenstain Bear Scouts Scream Their Heads Off	$3.50
☐ BBF94488-6	The Berenstain Bear Scouts and the Evil Eye	$3.50

© 1998 Berenstain Enterprises, Inc.

Available wherever you buy books or use this order form.